This book belongs to

....

Quarto is the authority on a wide range of topics.

Quarto educates, entertains and enriches the lives of our readers—enthusiasts and lovers of hands-on living.

www.quartoknows.com

© 2018 Quarto Publishing plc

First published in 2018 by QED Publishing, an imprint of The Quarto Group. The Old Brewery, 6 Blundell Street, London N7 9BH, United Kingdom. T (0)20 7700 6700 F (0)20 7700 8066 www.QuartoKnows.com

A catalogue record for this book is available from the British Library.

ISBN 978-1-78493-926-7

Based on the original story by Steve Smallman and Daniel Howarth
Author of adapted text: Katie Woolley
Series Editor: Joyce Bentley
Series Designer: Sarah Peden

Manufactured in Dongguan, China TL102017

9 8 7 6 5 4 3 2 1

MIX
Paper from responsible sources
FSC® C104723

Reading
Gems

The Grumpy Cat

Alf was a grumpy cat.
He never smiled.

Alf looked cross all the time.

Alf made the kittens sad. He made the other cats sad too.

When Alf looked very cross,
all the cats hid from him.

No one likes Alf.

The only time Alf looked happy
was when he was asleep.

That made Mum smile too.

One day the wind blew. It blew the leaves. It blew the cat's hat!

Alf liked the wind. It made him smile.

Alf's smile stuck! He was a happy cat.

He made the other cats happy too.

Alf's mum was asleep.

My smile
has stuck!

Mum smiled at Alf.

The other cats liked Alf now.
Alf smiled all the time.

No one hid from him.
Now Alf was very happy.

Alf was never grumpy again!

Story Words

asleep

blew

cat

cross

grumpy

happy

hat

hid

kitten

leaves

Mum

sad

smile

wind

Let's Talk About The Grumpy Cat

Look carefully at the book cover.

Who is the character on the cover?
Does he look friendly?

What is the weather like?
How can you tell?

Take a look at Alf in this picture.

What mood do you think he is in?

Can you find four other animals?

How do you think the other animals are feeling?

Was Alf happier at the beginning of the story or at the end?

This story is about being happy. What things make you happy?

Try pulling a grumpy face. Hold it!

Now try pulling a happy face. Which feels better and why?

How do you think Alf's mum felt when Alf was grumpy all the time?

How would your family and friends feel if you were always grumpy?

27

Fun and Games

Look at the pictures and words below.
Can you match each picture with its word?

hat   Mum   smile   cross

Answers: a: hat; b: smile; c: Mum; d: cross.

Look at the list of words below. How many times can you find each word in the book?

happy   grumpy   smile   Mum

Look at the expressions on the faces of the characters below. Match the words with how you think they are feeling.

scared   sad   happy

Your Turn

Now that you have read the story,
have a go at telling it in your own words.
Use the pictures below to help you.

GET TO KNOW READING GEMS

Reading Gems is a series of books that has been written for children who are learning to read. The books have been created in consultation with a literacy specialist.

The books fit into four levels, with each level getting more challenging as a child's confidence and reading ability grows. The simple text and fun illustrations provide gradual, structured practice of reading. Most importantly, these books are good stories that are fun to read!

Level 1 is for children who are taking their first steps into reading. Story themes and subjects are familiar to young children, and there is lots of repetition to build reading confidence.

Level 2 is for children who have taken their first reading steps and are becoming readers. Story themes are still familiar but sentences are a bit longer, as children begin to tackle more challenging vocabulary.

Level 3 is for children who are developing as readers. Stories and subjects are varied, and more descriptive words are introduced.

Level 4 is for readers who are rapidly growing in reading confidence and independence. There is less repetition on the page, broader themes are explored and plot lines straddle multiple pages.

The Grumpy Cat follows a cat who learns that it isn't always fun being grumpy. It explores themes of good behaviour, emotions and friendship.

Level 2

One day the wind blew. It blew the leaves. It blew the cat's hat!

Short sentences ✓

Some repetition ✓

Simple vocabulary ✓

Pictures and words support one another ✓